ISAAC

The Little Blue Dragon and The Stickiest Buns

There once was a young dragon.
He was short with two horns.
His tail was always waggin',
With blue scales that he adorns.

His teeth were like stars
And he walks on two feet.
He can open treat jars
And dances with the beat.

He is not very tall at all.
He's as big as you and me.
Isaac the dragon, you would call,
The happiest dragon you would see!

Isaac wears his hoodie of red
And his favorite black shorts.
"I am ready!", he eagerly said,
As if he was playing sports.

Isaac loves to eat sweet food
All from the baker's great store.
The baked goods always lift his mood.
That's why it's the best in Tudor.

His mom was ready for the store
And Isaac asked to come along.
With a smile, she invited him to Tudor
And off they went in song.

As they reached Tudor, the whole city was bustling.
The market was lively with people.
The townsfolk were shopping, eating, and hustling.
Truly a place no other could equal.

Trinkets and treats were usually sold,
Some of them bland and dull.
Some of them magic and very old
And others were just droll.

As they went shopping, a sweet scent arose.
It smelled of sugar & honey.
It was a scent that everyone knows.
Sticky buns all warm and sunny.

They trotted over to the famous bakery.
To find this tasty good.
On the sign it read, "Soul's Creamery"
The best food for your mood!

Isaac asked his mom for permission.
He really wanted a sticky bun.
She nodded and Isaac went on his mission.
He would not return until it was done.

As he entered the bakery, with money in hand,
The shop broke out in uproar.
The bakery was packed and every oven was manned.
It was quite a day for this sweets store.

The patrons were ordering every morsel in sight.
Not a baked good was safe from their hunger.
Isaac watched everyone enjoy their bite.
But luckily, his wait was no longer.

As he approached the counter, he was met with a smile.
"I'm Sarah the baker", she said.
"I'm the best baker within the mile
So please order more than bread."

Isaac searched the display for his tasty delight.
There were donuts, cakes and fudge.
Every sweet you could imagine was in his sight,
But nothing he saw made him budge.

"Excuse me, Miss!" he said with concern.
"What happened to all of your buns?"
Sarah looked in the case and said in return.
"That's funny. I thought we had tons."

Sarah turned to face Gary, her help in the kitchen.
"This wee dragon needs a warm bun".
With a crash, a pan came out of the oven
And then his rant begun...

17

"Every day the oven is hot,
Cookies and cakes are made.
Our sticky buns are sold nonstop,
But our hearts are never swayed."

18

"And yet there is always another customer
To desire our delicate sweets.
With a sweet tooth just like my big brother,
No wonder we run out of seats."

Gary looked all around within the case,
He even looked in the fridge.
He gave it his best detective face,
But he did not find a smidge.

Sadly Gary found none of those.
They were gone a while ago.
He searched the case and all of the rows,
But not a bun was left to show.

Isaac's face went straight to a frown
While the bad news echoed the room.
His empty stomach brought him down.
Nothing else could change his gloom.

22

Isaac turned to leave the shop
His head down in a slouch.
Before he could leave, Sarah asked him to stop
As she held a magic pouch.

"Are you sure?", Gary asked her with a grin.
Sarah whispered, "It's ours anyway".
Two sticky buns came from the pouch hidden,
And Isaac was overjoyed to pay.

With sticky buns in hand, he waved goodbye
To the baker, her assistant, and shop.
Isaac's mom asked him about his sweet buy,
And he showed her his sticky bun hop!

Soul's Creamery

Isaac's mom laughed as they shared a sweet bite,
And they giggled with glee and delight.
Everything worked out, and all was just right
And then they went home for a goodnight.

A Word from the Author

Thanks for reading my piece and I hope you enjoyed.
This next bit is a short poem that is not a part of the story.
I wrote it in the hopes that maybe someone would appreciate a
little word of reflection in these times.
Special thanks to my wife, Lauren, who had to hear me read
this...a lot.

Follow the Author:

Twitter: @hewithambitions
Instagram: @hewithambitions

"Price To Pay"

There's a price to pay for everything in life no
matter the context or day
Sometimes you pay it and sometimes you don't
but the price is here to stay
The price can be high. The price can be low.
But you only have so much to pay.

You pay to wake up and get out of bed.
You pay to show up and for every word that you
said.
Somebody had to listen to us today
And the price was in their head.

Somedays you'll have all the riches and more.
Somedays you'll scrape cents from your very core.
But every day you'll get something back
From your own personal tour.

So what you should do is manage it well
And avoid those folks with dreary spell
For your energy is all you have today
And to lose it would soon end your tale.

CPSIA information can be obtained
at www.ICGtesting.com
Printed in the USA
BVHW060511130721
611805BV00002B/28